A Ride in the Crummy

STORY BY **GARY HINES**

PICTURES BY
ANNA GROSSNICKLE HINES

Greenwillow Books New York

Watercolor paints were used
for the full-color art.
The text types are
Weiderman and Cochin.

Text copyright © 1991 by Gary Hines
Illustrations copyright © 1991
by Anna Grossnickle Hines
a division of William Morrow & Company, Inc.,
105 Madison Avenue, New York, NY 10016.
Printed in Singapore by Tien Wah Press
First Edition   10 9 8 7 6 5 4 3 2 1

Library of Congress Cataloging-in-Publication Data
Hines, Gary.
A ride in the crummy / by Gary Hines;
pictures by Anna Grossnickle Hines.
p   cm.
Summary: Two boys have an exciting ride
in the caboose of a big train.
ISBN 0-688-09691-3.
ISBN 0-688-09692-1 (lib. bdg.)
[1. Railroads — Trains — Fiction.]
I. Hines, Anna Grossnickle, ill.
II. Title.   PZ7.H5725Ri   1991
[E] — dc20   90-30848   CIP   AC

TO MOM, DAD, AND MANNY

"Here it comes, Grandpa!" Toby cried, as the sleek, silver train rolled into the station.

They clambered up the steps, and Toby hurried to find a seat next to a window.

Grandpa smiled. "Trains sure have changed since the 1930s, when I was a boy," he said, settling in next to his grandson. "But I used to get just as excited as you are. Why, I remember a *very* special trip. My little brother and I were standing next to the tracks. 'Here it comes!' I cried, just as you did...."

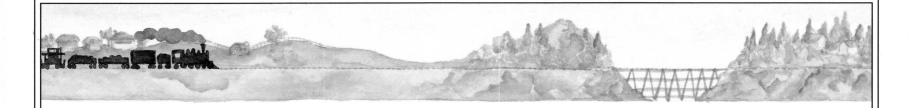

The giant, black steam engine chugged into the station. "Har-rumph!" went the locomotive, spitting out little clouds of white. Mama pulled us back out of the way.

We laughed excitedly. We were going to *ride* on that train. It would take us into the woods, where we would stay all summer while Papa worked in the logging camps.

One of the trainmen oiled the wheels. Those wheels were as big as I was. We waved at the engineer up in the cab.

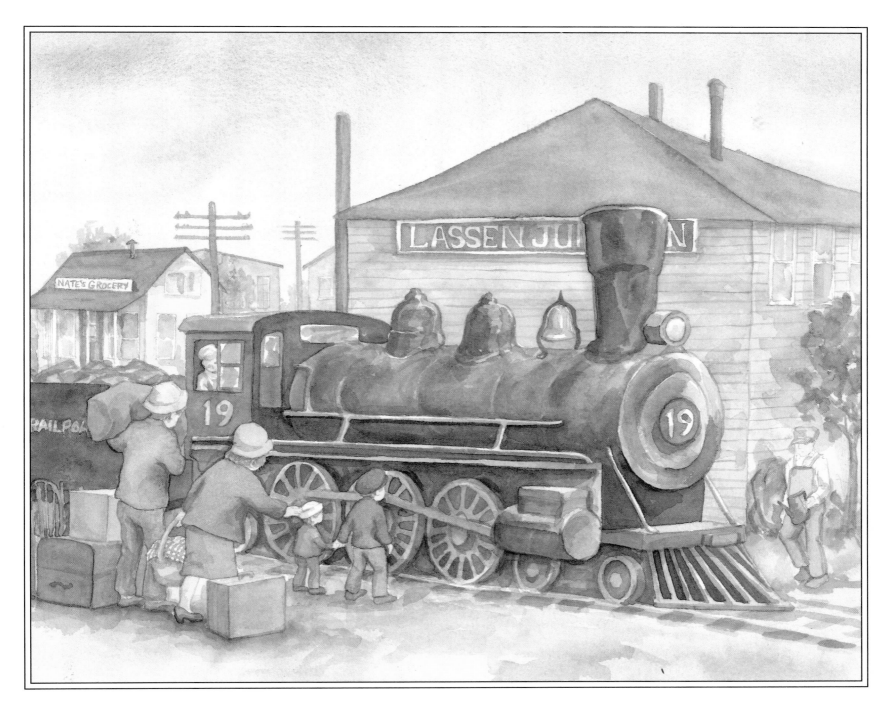

While Papa loaded our things, my brother and I ran back to the crummy. Mama had promised that this time we could sit in the high seats. A crummy is what men on the railroad called a caboose because it was so dirty with soot and grime.

Papa rode with the other men out on one of the flat cars.

The engineer blew the whistle. "Whoot! Whoot!" The train lurched forward. I grinned at my little brother.

"Kadunk-kathunk, kadunk-kathunk." The wheels spoke to the rails, slowly at first, then faster and faster. The steam engine huffed and puffed. "Huffa-puffa, huffa-puffa!" It painted the sky with smoke.

The depot slipped away, followed by lots of houses in town.

Then ranches and fences and cattle passed by. I waved to an old cow as the last farm disappeared behind us. Now hillsides with brush and green grass filled our windows.

The tracks got steeper. Trees with long needles reached out
to us. The giant locomotive slipped and spun its wheels.
"Akachoo-kachoo-kachoo!"

"Whoops!" I cried. "It's sneezing!" My brother laughed.

The wheels caught, and the engine chugged on again.
"Chuga-chuga, chuga-chuga."

At lunchtime Mama opened her basket and took out fried chicken, biscuits, and sliced pickles. We ate right on the train. It tasted good.

"Clickity-clack." Up the rails we went, hour after hour.

The train rolled. The train rocked. And it wiggled like a snake. We passed through tall places...and short places...and places so narrow we could almost touch the hillside.

On and on. Around and around. Up and up. The swaying caboose rocked more and more.

The locomotive blew its whistle again. This time it was long and loud! "Whooooooooooooo! Whoooooooooooooooooooooooo!" My brother and I plugged our ears.

"Here comes the 'Peeled Onion!'" someone called. That was the best part!

We jumped to the windows and looked out. Our eyes got big. We were on the side of a giant cliff! The tracks ran close to the edge, and it was a long, *long* way down.

"Whoa!" I yelled. A white river ran far below, and we looked down on the tops of trees growing in the canyon.

Suddenly the ground fell away, and all that was holding up that heavy train was a tall wooden trestle. "C-r-e-a-k!" went the trestle. "G-r-o-a-n!" went the trestle.

I closed my eyes. The trestle swayed, but I could still hear creaking and groaning as the wheels sang "kadonk-kathonk, kadonk-kathonk." I was glad when we made it across.

Tall, thick trees swallowed us up as the train chugged deeper into the forest. The sun flickered through the branches and across our eyes.

My brother pointed. Up ahead we could see some cabins peeking through the woods. The whistle blew again, and the train started to slow down.

"Here we are," Mama said, as she gathered up our things. Now we could see more cabins scattered around.

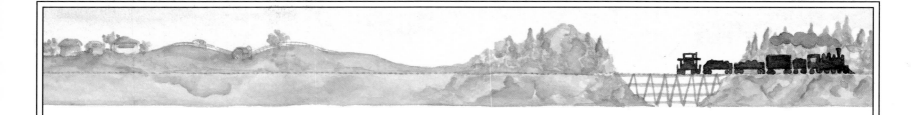

The brakes squeaked and squealed as the train ground to a stop. "Sounds like a piggy," I said.

We stepped off the caboose. While Mama and Papa got our stuff, my brother and I raced to the front of the train to look at the big steam engine one more time.

The engineer at the high window tugged on a cord. The whistle blew twice, and the empty train started forward. We waved, and the engineer smiled.

My little brother and I watched until the last car went out of sight.

"Those old steam trains sure were something," Grandpa said. "And I'll never forget that great ride, way up high in the crummy."